Cat Got a Lot

Steve Henry

I Like to Read®

Holiday House / New York

For Shelley

I LIKE TO READ® is a registered trademark of Holiday House, Inc.

Copyright © 2015 by Steve Henry
All Rights Reserved
HOLIDAY HOUSE is registered in the U.S. Patent and Trademark Office.
Printed and Bound in April 2015 at Tien Wah Press, Johor Bahru, Johor, Malaysia.
The artwork was created with watercolor, gouache ink and brown craft paper.
www.holidayhouse.com
First Edition
1 3 5 7 9 10 8 6 4 2

Library of Congress Cataloging-in-Publication Data
Henry, Steve, 1948-
Cat got a lot / Steve Henry. — First edition.
pages cm. — (I like to read)
Summary: "Cat goes out, and comes back with a lot of new things"— Provided by publisher.
ISBN 978-0-8234-3385-8 (hardcover)
[1. Cats—Fiction.] I. Title.
PZ7.H39732Cat 2015
[E]—dc23
2014032301

ISBN 978-0-8234-3419-0 (paperback)

Cat liked fish.

He went down.

And he went down.

Cat went out.

He saw a horn.

He went in.

Cat went out.

He saw books.

Cat went in.

And he went in.

And he went in.

Cat went back out.

And he went back in.

Then Cat went home.

And Cat was happy.